What Faust Saw

For Jacqueline

Copyright © 1995 by Matthew Ottley
All rights reserved.
CIP Data is available.
Published in the United States 1996 by Dutton Children's Books,
a division of Penguin Books USA Inc.
375 Hudson Street, New York, New York 10014
Originally published in Australia and New Zealand 1995
by Hodder Headline Australia Pty Limited
Display typography by Julia Goodman
Designed by Liz Seymour
Printed in Hong Kong
First American Edition
ISBN 0-525-45650-3
1 2 3 4 5 6 7 8 9 10

What Faust Saw

MATT OTTLEY

Dutton Children's Books • *New York*

One night Faust woke up, looked out the window, and . . .

. . . saw something *very* strange.

He tried to wake up Mom . . . *and* Isabelle . . . *and* Clayton . . .

. . . *even* Dad.

But they didn't seem to want to WAKE UP.

Faust hid.

That woke up Dad.

Dad looked everywhere.

Well, almost everywhere.

"Bad dog!" said Dad.

He locked Faust outside.

Poor Faust.

Soon he was back inside.

"Bad, **bad** dog!"

said Mom.

"Outside again!"

"Bad, bad, bad, bad dog!"

said Dad and Mom and Isabelle and Clayton.

Now Faust was getting ANGRY. It wasn't *his* fault.

He decided to *run away*.
Then they'd be sorry.

But he was followed . . . .

Someone else heard him bark, too.

Faust FLED.

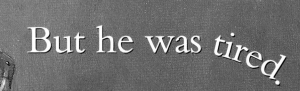

But he was tired.

After all, he hadn't had much sleep.

"Off to the pound with you," said the dog catcher. "No strays allowed in *this* neighborhood."

The **next** morning Dad *and* Mom *and* Isabelle *and* Clayton came to the pound.

EXHIBITION

LIFE ON OTHER PLANETS

MUSE

Faust decided to forgive them and go home.

He **also** decided that the **next** time he woke up and saw something **strange** . . .

. . . he would go back to sleep.